DEDICATED TO OUR

FAVORITE MONSTERS

LITTLE BIGFOOT

HIDE-AND-SEEK

BY ALICIA VAN GOTTEN

It's a bright, sunny day
Little Bigfoot is ready to play!

Breakfast is a yummy bagel.
Little Bigfoot hides under the table.

Running through the forest, filled with glee,
Little Bigfoot hides behind a tree

The river is home to fish and frog.
Little Bigfoot hides like a floating log.

The sun is setting, it's getting colder.
Little Bigfoot hides behind a boulder.

He can hear his mama call.
Little Bigfoot hides behind the waterfall.

Home at last, after some grub,
Little Bigfoot hides in the big bathtub.

Time to lay down his sleepy head,
Little Bigfoot hides in his snuggly bed.

Made in the USA
Monee, IL
16 November 2020